Usborne

A Sticker Dolly Story
Lucky Bunnies

Zanna Davidson

Illustrated by Sylwia Filipczak
Cover illustration by Antonia Miller

Use the stickers to dress the Dolls on the 'Meet the Dolls' pages

Meet the
Animal Rescue Dolls

Zoe, Amelia and Jack are the 'Animal Rescue Dolls'. They look after the animals that live on the Wild Isle, helping animals in trouble and caring for any that are injured.

Amelia

has a special bond with dogs and rabbits. She also adores having pets of her own.

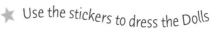

Use the stickers to dress the Dolls

Jack

has a passion for sea
creatures. He is also
a keen birdwatcher
and is never without
his binoculars.

Zoe

is brilliant at working
with wild horses and
loves riding. She is also
fascinated by reptiles.

Dolly Town

The Animal Rescue Dolls work at the Animal Sanctuary, in Dolly Town, home to all the Dolls. The Dolls work in teams to help those in trouble and are the very best at what they do, whether that's animal rescue, magical missions or protecting the planet. Each day brings with it an exciting new adventure…

The **Shooting Star** train whisks the Dolls away on their missions.

Madame Coco's **Costume Emporium** has everything the Dolls might need.

The Dolls love to celebrate at the **Cupcake Café.**

The **Animal Sanctuary** is where the Animal Rescue Dolls work.

Rose Theatre

Bluebell Bookshop

Evergreen Sports Arena

Royal Palace

Palm Tree
Film Studios

Fashion Design
Studio

Heartbeat
Dance Academy

Mission Control Centre
lets the Dolls know
who's in trouble and
where to go.

Pop Star
Stadium

Silver Sparkles
Skating Rink

Strawberry
Lane Stables

Honeysuckle Cottage

Chapter One

A Busy Week

"What a busy week!" said Zoe, as they all sat around the little table at the Animal Sanctuary. "First we had to deliver the twin lambs…"

"And help the baby birds that had fallen out of their nests," added Jack.

"And then the rescue rabbits arrived," said Amelia, looking down at two floppy-eared bunnies, snuggled up in their hutch. "Aren't they gorgeous?"

"They're really sweet!" said Zoe.

"Have you thought of names for them yet, Amelia?"

"Of course I have," Amelia replied with a grin. "The spotty one is Bouncer, because she does such big bouncy jumps, and the brown and white one is Honey. I'm going to start looking for a new home for them today. I really hope I find one quickly – and that they can stay together."

Amelia began fluffing up the bedding, but just then, her mission watch started to flash.

"Looks like we have a new mission coming in!" she called to the others. Jack reached over and picked up his screen. "Come in, Mission Control," he said.

"We need all three Animal Rescue Dolls," replied Mission Control. "Are you there?"

"Yes, we're all here," said Zoe, as everyone gathered round.

There's been
a flood on
the Wild Isle,
in the Wildflower Meadows
to the south. And it's causing
a problem for the bunnies...

"Oh no!" said Amelia. "Are
they okay?"

"They're all sitting on a small
hill to the north of the meadow.
They're safe for now, but the
water is rising fast and there's

nowhere else for them to go. Can you help?"

"We're on the case!" said Jack. "We'll be there as soon as we can."

"Sending through the mission details now."

Mission to the Wildflower Meadows

Mission facts:

The river above the Wildflower Meadows has burst its banks.

The bunnies were last seen on the top of the hill.

They need to be rescued, and soon, as the current is strong and the water is rising fast.

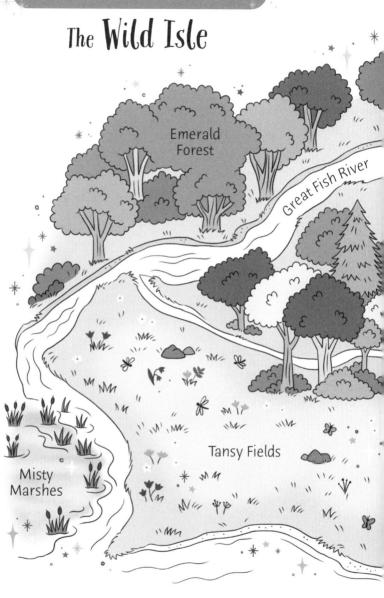

MISSION LOCATION:

The **Wild Isle**

Emerald
Forest

Great Fish River

Tansy Fields

Misty
Marshes

Horseshoe
Cove

Wildflower
Meadows

*The bunnies
were last
seen here*

RABBIT RESCUE:

The rabbits on the Wild Isle are mostly grey-brown, but sometimes there are black rabbits.

Around twenty rabbits live in the warren in the Wildflower Meadows.

Some of the rabbits will have had babies recently. Their kittens will be in especial danger.

There's a chance some rabbits may have been swept away by the water, so keep an eye out for any missing bunnies.

WILD RABBIT FEATURES:

Long, straight ears

Sensitive whiskers

Fluffy, white tail

Long hind legs

Baby bunnies are called kittens.

"Mission received," said Amelia.

The Animal Rescue Dolls turned and looked at each other.

"I'll feed the lambs," said Zoe.

"I'll check on all the birds," said Jack.

"And I'll make sure the animals have water," added Amelia. "Then it'll be Mission Go!"

The Animal Rescue Dolls hurried around the sanctuary, feeding and watering the animals.

Then they all met by the front door.

"Right," said Zoe. "First stop…"

Chapter Two

A Trip to Madame Coco's

The Animal Rescue Dolls strode across the street to Madame Coco's. Outside, a fresh spring breeze stirred the air, while birds swooped overhead.

At Madame Coco's, the window boxes were full of flowers, from brightest blues to sunshine yellows.

On any other day, the Dolls would be stopping to admire the colours, but today they raced through the revolving door and made their way to the famous glass elevator.

"Good afternoon!" said Jasper, the lift attendant, smiling at them from under his peaked cap. "Where can I take you today?"

"Floor number three, please," said Zoe. "We're on an urgent mission."

The Dolls stepped inside the lift, Jasper pressed the button and the doors swished shut. Then the lift glided up and up, before coming to a stop with a gentle

TING!

"Thank you!" called Amelia, as the Rescue Dolls stepped out into a large, airy room, filled with everything they could need for travelling to rocky mountains, lush wetlands and sandy deserts.

"Ah! Welcome, Animal Rescue Dolls," came a soft voice, and they turned to see Madame Coco gliding towards them, looking as elegant as ever in a floral skirt, with a silk scarf threaded through her hair. "Are you here on a mission?"

"We are," said Amelia. "A river has burst its banks on the Wild Isle, and some rabbits are trapped on a little hill. Our mission is to take them to dry land, and to search for any in the water."

"Then I know exactly what you'll need," said Madame Coco.

A moment later, she was whirling around the room, her assistants hurrying in her wake, as she pulled out gleaming boots, well-cut jackets and fluffy blankets…

Amelia's clothes

A purple
waxed jacket

White polka
dot blouse

Shiny black
waterproof boots

Jade green trousers
with embroidery

"Here you are!" she said, as the assistants handed the Dolls their clothes. "For Amelia – knee-high boots to keep the water out – and stylish too! Your trousers are made out of my favourite material – so thin and light but they'll keep you warm and dry.

Trekking trousers for you, Jack – a perfect fit – and hiking boots.

As for you, Zoe – a pair of sleek, shiny leggings, that are water-resistant too, and boots with thick, chunky soles. I always say that

Zoe's clothes

Striped green and white top

Bottle green jacket with drawstring waist

Black leggings in soft, stretchy fabric

Waterproof lace-up boots

Jack's clothes

Cargo trousers
with zip pockets

Light beige fleece and
white knitted top

Waterproof
hiking boots

even the most functional clothes
can be fashionable."

Then the Dolls stepped into the
changing rooms…

…and when they stepped out again, they were dressed and ready for their mission.

Madame Coco handed each of them a rucksack, full to the brim with kit. "There are quick drying blankets, in case any of the rabbits get wet, a first-aid kit for small mammals, a net to help you catch the rabbits, and boxes and bedding to transport them.

And this…" she added, handing them a large brown canvas bag.

"Ooh! What's inside?" asked Amelia.

"A pack raft," said Madame Coco. "In case the water gets too deep, with life vests for you all."

"Wow! Thank you!" said Jack. "You really do think of everything."

"And I have two more things for you…" Madame Coco went on. She went over to a little cupboard marked 'A Touch of Magic', and pulled out three tiny sweet-smelling bags, that sparkled in the light.

"These were a gift from the Magic Dolls – a special concoction of rose petals, lemon balm, chickweed and lavender…and a pinch of sparkle dust.

I call it *Calming Confetti*. Sprinkle
this over the wild bunnies if you
need to calm them. And last but
not least…"

Madame Coco held up a forked
hazel twig.

"Is it a wand?" asked Zoe.

"Not quite," replied Madame Coco, "although it is a present from the Magic Dolls. They tell me that hazel has magical properties and can help you to look for anything that's lost. Hazel works especially well around water. If you hold out this twig and chant what you want to find, it should lead you to it."

Amelia took it, smiling gratefully. "This will be a huge help," she said.

"I hope so," Madame Coco
replied. "Bunnies are my favourite
animal, after all."

"I didn't know that," said
Amelia, as they turned to go.

"I've always wanted pet ones,"
sighed Madame Coco, "but I was
worried I didn't have enough space
for them. However, I've been
working on a little project…and
now, at last, I know *exactly* where
I can keep them!"

Amelia's face lit up. "I've got two rescue rabbits, ready for re-homing. They're called Bouncer and Honey."

"Oh!" said Madame Coco, smiling. "*Vraiment?*" she said. "Really?"

"I'll send you photographs of them," called Amelia, as she went to join the others.

"Thank you!" Madame Coco called back. "That sounds perfect. I'd love to give them a home."

"In that case, I'll be in touch after the mission!" said Amelia.

With a final
wave, the Animal
Rescue Dolls
whizzed back
down in the lift

TING!

and out onto
the sunny street.
Zoe tapped
her watch to
summon the
Shooting Star,
and in no time

at all, it drew up beside
them in a glittering cloud.

"Hello, Animal Rescue Dolls," said
Sienna, the train driver. "I'm guessing
you need to go to the Wild Isle?"

"Yes please," said Jack. "To the
little hill to the north of the
Wildflower Meadows."

"Step aboard," said Sienna.
"I'll have you there in no time."

The train doors closed and the Shooting Star sped away, whizzing through Dolly Town before entering a dark tunnel, glimmering with hundreds of tiny lights.

With a

WHOOSH

they shot out the other side.

Before them lay the Wild Isle, glinting like a jewel in the spring sunshine.

The Shooting Star wound its way across the Misty Marshes and Tansy Fields before arriving at the edge of the Wildflower Meadows…

"Oh no!" gasped Zoe, gazing at the meadows. "I hadn't realized the flood would be this bad!"

"Look how high the water line is!" added Jack. "The water's even starting to flood onto Tansy Fields. Some of the flowers are half-submerged!"

"I'll have to pull up here," said Sienna, coming to a halt by a line of trees. "I can't make it any further. The trees are too closely packed together."

"Thank you, Sienna," said the Dolls, as one by one they stepped off the train onto a ridge that ran alongside the flooded meadow.

As the Shooting Star pulled away, Jack peered through his binoculars, searching for the bunnies.

There, on the other side of the meadow, on a little hill that was now the last patch of dry land, were the bunnies. And all around them the water was rising fast…

Chapter Three
The Stranded Bunnies

The Animal Rescue Dolls
exchanged anxious glances.

"Rabbits can swim, can't they?"
said Zoe, taking a
look through
Jack's binoculars.

"They can,"
said Amelia,

"but the current must be too strong for them. We'll need to catch them and then take them to safe ground."

"In that case," said Jack, "let's get Rabbit Rescue underway! And three cheers for Madame Coco! We'll definitely be needing that raft…"

On those words, he began unzipping the canvas bag she had given them. Zoe put together the pump and as soon as Jack had laid out the raft, she began to inflate it.

"There are paddles, too," said
Amelia, slotting them together.

When the raft was ready, they
put on their life vests and climbed
aboard. Jack and Zoe began to row
towards the little hill, while Amelia
unpacked the carrier boxes, ready
for the bunnies.

"I'm looking, but I can't see any

bunnies in the water," said Jack.

"Nor can I," added Amelia.
"Perhaps they're all safe on the hill.
We'll have to approach really quietly
so as not to scare them. I think each
box should fit about three bunnies.
We can close the lids, as there are

holes for air, and the rabbits will feel calmer in the dark."

"Catching them might be difficult," said Jack. "Bunnies are super fast!"

"We've got Madame Coco's *Calming Confetti* for that," Amelia reminded him. "Hopefully that will make catching the bunnies easier."

By now, they'd arrived at the mound of dry earth poking up above the water. Zoe tied a rope around a tree trunk to secure the raft, and they climbed ashore,

keeping their movements
as slow and gentle as
they could.

The bunnies were huddled together at the top of the mound, their little bodies shivering in the cold air.

"Oh poor things," said Zoe.

"Let's count them," said Jack.

Mission Control said there should be around twenty bunnies.

"I can only see thirteen," said Amelia, counting beneath her breath. "And there's no sign of any babies. Where could the others be?"

"I don't know," said Jack, looking around at the rising water.

Worryingly, it was already lapping at their ankles. "But shall we make a start with these ones?"

"Good idea," said Amelia. "We'll need these nets to catch them," she added, handing them round.

But even though the Dolls approached as quietly as they could, the bunnies began to scatter.

"Quick!" said Zoe. "Let's use our *Calming Confetti*. I really hope it works. We don't have long."

They each took out their little bags and began sprinkling the confetti over the bunnies.

At once, the air was filled with
the scent of wild flowers and a
glittering dust that shimmered as
it fell. As soon as it touched the
bunnies, they stopped running
and grew calm and still.

"Oh, this is amazing," said Jack. "We don't even need these nets. The bunnies are just letting me pick them up."

One by one, they scooped up the wet, cold bunnies, before putting them carefully in the boxes.

"This is the last one I can see,"

said Zoe, giving the bunny in her arms a quick rub with a towel to dry it off, before placing it snugly in a box with the others. "But we're still missing some bunnies," she said. "The water's getting higher and higher! We really don't have long to find them!"

"Maybe the mission details were wrong?" said Jack, looking back over the mound.

"I can't see any bunnies in the water," added Zoe, "and there definitely aren't any more here."

"Wait a moment!" said Amelia, her voice filled with anxiety. "There are some holes over here. This mound must be the warren! We just didn't realize it because all the entrances are underwater…except these ones."

"Do you think the missing bunnies are underground?" asked Zoe.

"Yes! *That's* where the kittens must be!" said Amelia. "Little babies are too young to leave the burrow. They could still be inside, unable to get out…and the water's still rising. If we don't act fast, they'll be drowned."

Chapter Four

Baby Bunnies

"What can we do?" asked Jack.
"We won't have time to
check all of these burrows.
The water's already beginning to
trickle in…"

"The hazel twig!" said Zoe,
remembering suddenly. "Do you
think it could help us find the

missing bunnies? Madame Coco did say it has the power to find lost things, and that it's especially powerful near water? And we're *definitely* surrounded by water!"

Amelia pulled the hazel twig from her bag and held it over the mound.

"Find the missing bunnies," she muttered beneath her breath, her words coming out like a chant.

"Find the missing bunnies!"

She didn't really believe that anything would happen, but to her amazement, she felt at once as if the twig was pulling her towards one of the burrows.

It was as if a strange fizzing feeling were travelling all the way from the twig and up her arm, telling her that the baby bunnies were near.

"Down there," said Amelia, pointing. "That's where the baby bunnies are!"

"Are you sure?" asked Jack, looking on in amazement.

Amelia nodded. "I've got such a strong feeling," she said. "I just *know* there are some tiny little rabbits down there." She closed her eyes. "I can picture them…their little noses twitching, their eyes wide with fear…"

72

Swiftly, Zoe lay on the ground
and reached her arm down the hole.

"Can you feel them?" asked Amelia.

"No..." said Zoe. "There's
nothing there."

"I'm *sure* there is," said Amelia.

Zoe stretched her arm even further.

"Oh yes!" she cried suddenly, as her

fingertips brushed soft fur.

"You'll have to be quick," said Jack. Looking down, he could see the water would soon start to flood the burrows.

Zoe nodded, and as carefully as she could, she cupped her hand around the soft baby bunny and pulled it out, placing it gently into Jack's cupped hands. Then she went back for the next one.

The baby bunny blinked at the sudden daylight and tried to wriggle away, but Jack held it safe.

Zoe brought out four more.
They were so tiny, Jack was able to
hold them all at once.

"Is that it?" asked Jack.

"I can't feel any more," said Zoe, lying down one more time on the waterlogged ground.

"I'll check," said Amelia, and she held the hazel twig over the burrow. "That's it," she agreed, nodding. "I'm not getting any sense that we've left any behind."

"But Mission Control said there were twenty bunnies," Jack replied, "and we've only got nineteen."

"They only said *around* twenty," Amelia pointed out. "And we really do need to leave now. We're going

to be underwater soon…"

Even as she spoke, a wave of water washed over the very top of the mound, taking the last patch of dry land with it.

Jack placed the baby bunnies in a fresh box lined with hay.

They all put on their life vests,
then Zoe and Amelia began to
row away, while Jack kept a
careful eye on the boxes full of
precious bunnies.

"It's hard work rowing against
this current," said Amelia, looking

down at the swirling waters. "And we need to find a safe place to re-home these rabbits. However cosy we've made them, they'll be feeling stressed and anxious once Madame Coco's *Calming Confetti* wears off. I want to get them to dry land as soon as possible."

"From what I remember," said Jack, "there's an old warren among the trees that's been empty for a

while now. It's higher ground there, so it won't be flooded. Shall we try it?"

"That sounds like a great plan," said Zoe.

At once, Amelia and Zoe began rowing hard and fast towards the tree line, their paddles moving together in one fluid motion.

But then Jack spotted a dark shape floating in the water.

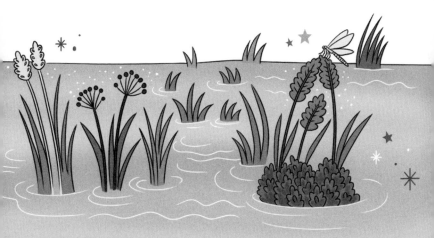

"Stop!" he cried. "To your right – there's something in the water. I think…oh no…I think it's a black bunny. And it's not moving!"

Immediately, Zoe plunged her paddle into the water, turning the boat. Amelia lay on her stomach, stretching out until the bunny was within reach. Then she pulled it from the water into her arms.

The bunny lay there, soaking
wet and very still.

Amelia placed her hand on his
side. "He's breathing," she said.
"He's definitely still breathing."

"Oh, poor little thing," said Zoe.
"He must have been trying to
swim across, but the current got
too strong for him."

"Do you think he's going to make it?" asked Jack.

"It's touch and go," said Amelia. "But I'll do everything I can to save him."

Chapter Five
The Black Bunny

A melia put the bunny in the recovery position and began gently rubbing him with one of the towels. "He's really cold," she said. "The most important thing is to warm him up." She bent down. "Come on, little bunny," she urged.

They all waited for a few tense
moments, while the bunny lay
very still. Then, at last, his ears
twitched and he began to make
little noises.

"That's a good sign," said Amelia. "I think he's going to be okay."

She wrapped the bunny in the towel and then put him under her top. "This will keep him warm," she said. "Now, let's keep rowing!"

With swift strokes, Jack and Zoe rowed to the bank on the other side. By the time they had climbed out of the raft, the black bunny was wriggling away under Amelia's top, making her laugh.

"We can release the rabbits here," said Amelia. "They'll be safe from the flood waters and there's lots of grass to feed on. And just as Jack said – I can see an abandoned warren over there. A readymade home!"

Zoe carefully lifted the boxes from the raft and placed them on the dry ground. Opening the boxes, she smiled as the rabbits popped up their heads to look at their new surroundings, ears pricked, eyes bright.

For a moment, the Animal Rescue Dolls were surrounded by boxes full of bunnies, their bodies now warm and soft from being nestled in the hay.

Then, one by one, they began to venture out.

Some were bold and bounded away immediately, their fluffy white tails shining in the sunlight. Others were more tentative, waiting a moment before hopping away.

"Oh, look at those ones!" said Zoe, pointing and smiling at a group of young rabbits, jumping and leaping as if overjoyed to be free again.

"What shall we do with the babies?" asked Jack.

"Let's put them in one of the abandoned burrows," said Amelia. "We'll just have to hope the mother picks up the scent and returns to them. Mother bunnies only feed their babies twice a day, so she might not go back to them straightaway."

Zoe popped the baby bunnies in the abandoned warren, along with their nesting material to keep them warm.

"If the mother doesn't go to them, we'll have to take them back with us," said Amelia, "but I really hope she returns. Their mother's milk is the best thing for them."

"What about the black bunny?" asked Jack.

"I've put him in one of the boxes," said Amelia. "I wanted to make sure he really is okay before releasing him."

As she spoke, she bent down and peeked under the lid. "Yes," she said, laughing, "he's definitely okay!

He's nibbling on the hay and his fur is all fluffed up again."

The others bent down to look. "Isn't he gorgeous?" said Jack.

"He is," agreed Amelia. "Right, time to join the others, my little friend."

She lifted the lid and, after a moment, the black bunny bounded away.

"And look!" cried Zoe. "Over there! I think that's the mother bunny going to see her kittens."

They all looked as a rabbit sniffed the air, as if following a trail to the burrow. She paused for a moment at the entrance and then hopped inside.

"Oh, I hope that *is* the mother, and that she's feeding them," said Amelia.

Jack picked up his binoculars and walked over to get a better look. Then he flicked his binoculars into night-vision mode, so he could see into the burrow. "We're in luck!" he said, with a grin. "She's definitely feeding them."

The Animal Rescue Dolls turned and smiled at each other.

"Mission accomplished," said Zoe, gazing around at the happy

rabbits, lolloping between the trees.
"Time to call the Shooting Star."

As she spoke, she tapped the
symbol on her watch. Soon, the
Shooting Star train was gliding
towards the little clearing in a

cloud of shimmering dust.

"Well done, Animal Rescue Dolls," said Sienna. "I can see you've safely rescued the bunnies. Where would you like to go now?"

"The Cupcake Café please, to celebrate," said Jack. "I think we could all do with a hot chocolate to warm us up!"

But Amelia looked at them pleadingly. "Could we go to the Animal Sanctuary first?" she said.

"I sent Madame Coco a photograph of Honey and Bouncer and she said she'd love to have them. Can we take them to their new home?"

"Definitely," said Zoe. "After all, it's a day for lucky bunnies!"

Chapter Six

Bunny Heaven!

I n no time at all, the Shooting Star had whisked Amelia, Jack and Zoe back to the Animal Sanctuary in Dolly Town.

"Thank you!" called the Dolls, as Sienna pulled away in another glittering cloud of dust.

After a quick stop at the

Sanctuary, all three Dolls were soon standing at the entrance to Madame Coco's – only this time, Amelia had two rescue bunnies in a shiny blue pet carrier.

They stepped through the revolving door to be met by Madame Coco, who was waiting for them excitedly.

"Oh! You've brought the rabbits!" she said

"We have," said Zoe. "Amelia couldn't wait! But where will you be keeping them?" she asked, looking around at the immaculate shop floor.

"Don't worry," said Madame Coco. "I have that all worked out. Follow me."

She led them to the lift and
smiled at Jasper, giving him a
little nod.

"Ah!" said Jasper. "I'll take you
to the secret floor!"

He unlatched a hidden door in
the lift panel and pressed a button.

The lift whizzed
up and up,
passing floor
after floor.

"Where are
we going?"
asked Jack.

"The roof
garden!" said
Madame Coco, a
glint in her eye,
as the lift gently
came to a halt.

TING!

The doors swished open to reveal
a beautiful garden, full of grass and
flowers, with a fence all around,
covered in sweet-smelling roses.

Against one of the walls stood a large hutch, full of fresh hay, with a little ramp down to the garden and a bowl full of bunny food inside.

"Oh wow!" said Amelia, laughing. "This is rabbit heaven!"

"I know!" said Madame Coco, smiling back at her. "It's completely secure, so the rabbits will have the garden to themselves by day, and a snug hutch to keep them warm at night. And plenty of attention from me too, of course!"

Amelia bent down and opened the carrier to let out Honey and Bouncer.

"Welcome to your new home," said Madame Coco, giving them some fresh greens.

"They're going to love it here," said Zoe, beaming.

"And I have another surprise for you all," said Madame Coco. "As a way of saying thank you for the rabbits, I decided to bring the Cupcake Café to *you*, for once."

"To *us*?" queried Jack.

Madame Coco gestured to a pretty screen at the back of the roof garden. Two of her assistants rolled it back, to reveal an outdoor table and chairs, and Maya standing there smiling at them all.

"Welcome to the Rooftop Cupcake Café!" said Maya, laughing. "We've got biscuits, cakes and most important of all, hot chocolates brimming with marshmallows!"

"And let's not forget…bunnies!" added Amelia, as they took their seats, Honey and Bouncer happily hopping around beside them.

Then the Rescue Dolls raised their cups of hot chocolate and chinked them together. "Animal Rescue Dolls forever!" they said in unison.

The End

Join the **Animal Rescue Dolls** on their next adventure in

Usborne
A Sticker Dolly Story
Little Lost Deer

with stickers

Zanna Davidson

Read on for a sneak peek...

Z oe hurried over to the table and picked up her olive green tablet, tapping on the flashing paw print.

"Mission Control here!" came a voice. "Are the Animal Rescue Dolls there?"

"Yes, we're all here," said Zoe.

"What's happening?"

"I'm afraid there's trouble on the Wild Isle. A fire has spread through the Emerald Forest. Don't worry, the fire has gone out now, and no animals were harmed, but a mother deer has been seen, wandering the forest without any sign of her fawn.

We think she could have been separated from her mother in the fire and become lost. The fawn would only be about a week old and she needs her mother's milk."

"The poor little fawn," said Amelia. "I do hope she's okay. She must have been so worried

by the fire. Of course we'll help."

"We'll do everything we can to find the fawn," added Jack.

"Sending through the mission details now," said Mission Control.

"Thank you!" said Zoe. "We'll be there as soon as we can. It's Mission Go!"

The rescue mission and events in this book are entirely fictional and should never be attempted by anyone other than a trained professional.

Edited by Lesley Sims and Stephanie King
Designed by Hannah Cobley and Hope Reynolds
Additional design by Johanna Furst and Jacqui Clark
Additional illustrations by Heather Burns
Expert advice from Suzanne Rogers

First published in 2022 by Usborne Publishing Ltd.,
Usborne House, 83-85 Saffron Hill, London EC1N 8RT, England.
usborne.com Copyright © 2022 Usborne Publishing Ltd. UKE